MeOW
IS NOT A
CAT

Kelly Tills
Max Saladrigas

Dedicated to the most unpredictable person on earth. -Kelly

Always to M. -Max

A division of FDI publishing LLC

Hi, I'm
Meow.

Not him, me! I'm not a cat.

I'm not really sure why
everyone calls me Meow.

Maybe it's because I get bored easily.

Maybe it's because of my adorable charm.

Maybe it's the hat?

Or maybe it's because
I dance like a flat-footed duck on a hotplate.

Cats don't do that.

People say cats don't listen.
My teacher, Ms. Snickety, says that about me too.

Not true. I just listen differently. Like if a sign points to
the left, that means go left. It doesn't say to walk left,
be quiet, and stay in line.

It doesn't *say* not to stuff the sign in my hat, squawk like a pterodactyl, and fly to the left singing...

TWEEDLE-DEE
TWEEDLE-DUM
TOOTLE POODLE
DONKEY BUTT

What?

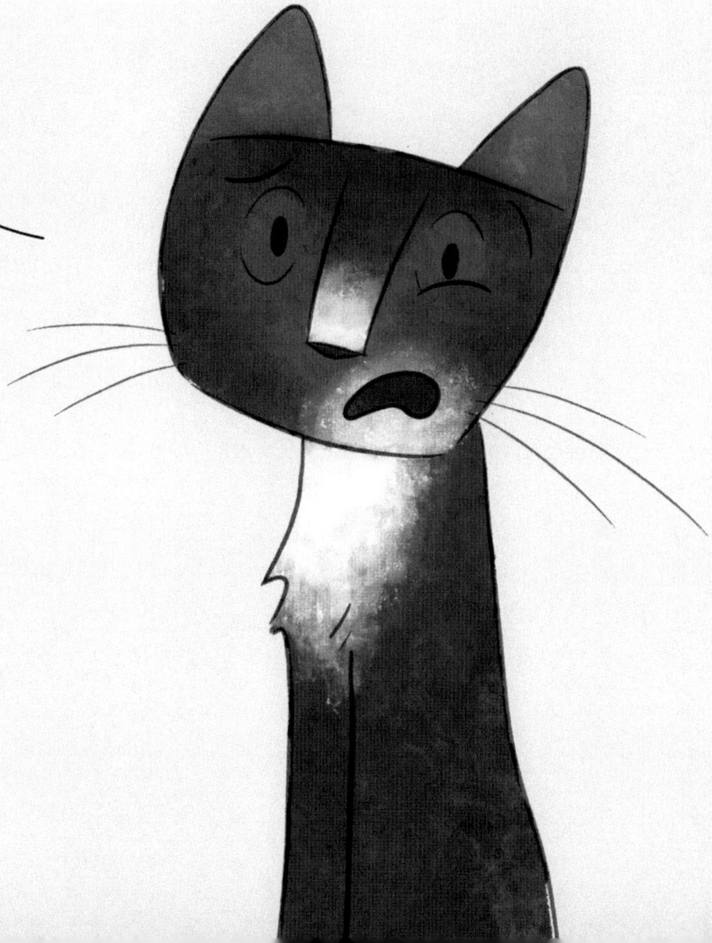

Ms. Snickety loses her patience with me a lot. "Oh, Meow, will you please just get in line," she says, "It's like herding cats."

"I'm not a cat, MS. Snickety. Cats lick their butts."

Ms. Snickety likes lines.

"Chip chop, let's go,"

she says before an outing.

So I do a little chip chop. But I guess that's not what she means. Why not just say "get in line?"

Ms. Snickety doesn't need patience with the other kids.

They line up right.   They play right.   They sing right.

When I try, it all comes out different.

Today we went on an outing to feed the monkeys. There were monkeys everywhere. Ms. Snickety gave each kid some bananas and said, "If you hold them out, the monkeys will jump for them."

They sure *did* jump for them. At first it was fun. But then the monkeys swiped all the bananas and there were none left for the kids.

That's not fair! The monkeys weren't sharing.
But Ms. Snickety always says,

"Sharing is caring."

So when a monkey jumped for *my* banana, I yanked it
away. "How about we share?" I asked.

They didn't understand.

I was going to have to show them. "Here, like this," I said, and I grabbed a couple of bananas to give back to the kids. That made the monkeys mad.

I started grabbing up more and more bananas. The next thing I knew, I had *all* the bananas, and *all* the monkeys were chasing me.

This was not the plan. I needed those monkeys to stop!
Ms. Snickety always says,

"Monkey see, monkey do"

so...

I stopped.

I did not see that coming.

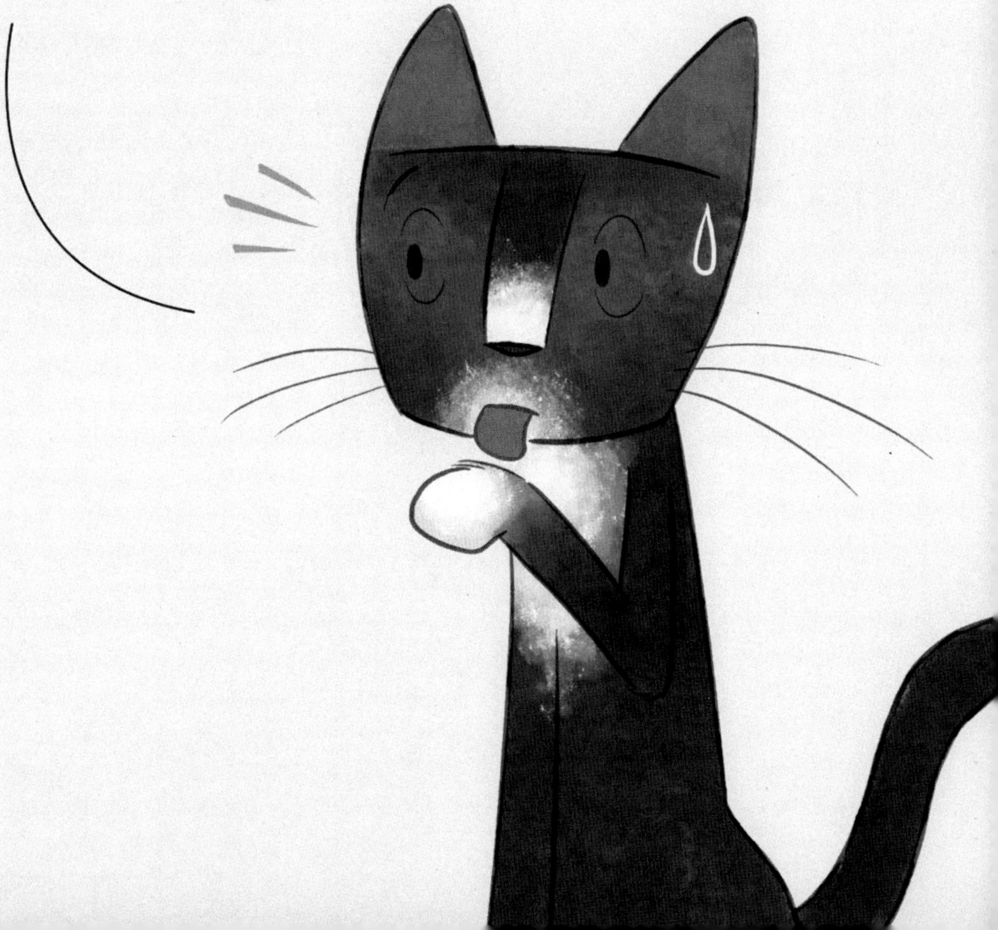

And they stopped.
It worked!

Until they remembered

they were mad

(and I still had all the bananas).

I needed a new plan.

I may dance like a duck,
but I can also leap like a frog.

I needed to get away fast.
I frog-leaped to the left. I duck-danced to the right.

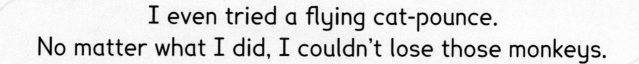

I even tried a flying cat-pounce.
No matter what I did, I couldn't lose those monkeys.

Hmmm, if I had just stayed in line...

AH-HA!

I shouted as loud as I could,
"Everybody,
GET IN LINE!"

The other kids got right back into line. They sure are good at that. "Don't let the monkeys get through," I shouted. "This time, everybody gets a banana!"

Even Ms. Snickety got one.
"Oh Meow, where do you get these ideas?" she asked.

"I was just doing what you always say,"
I answered, "It just comes out different."

And you know what she did next?

About the Author

Kelly Tills writes silly books for kids and believes even the smallest hat-tip, in the simplest books, can teach our kids how to approach the world. Kelly's children's stories are perfect to read aloud to young children, or to let older kids read themselves (hey, let them flex those new reading skills!). Proud member of the *International Dyslexia Association.*

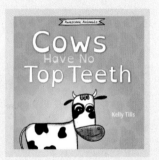

Check out Kelly's *Awesome Animals* series. Each book explores one fun fact, about one animal, and contains one key vocabulary word like "slither", "evaporate" or "graze." Silly science, perfect for ages 0-5 and emerging readers up to 2nd grade.

I hope you had as much fun reading this book as I had writing it. Don't forget to leave a review!

Go to kellytills.com/meow
or point your phone's camera here.
It'll take you straight to the review page.
Magic!

Made in the USA
Middletown, DE
14 April 2022

64134629R00024